BENJY

a ferocious fairy tale

EDWIN O'CONNOR

BENJY

a ferocious fairy tale

Pictures by
CATHARINE O'NEILL

A Pocket Paragon from
DAVID R. GODINE PUBLISHER
Boston

First U.S. edition published in 1996 by
DAVID R. GODINE, PUBLISHER, INC.
P. O. Box 9103
Lincoln, Massachusetts 01773

Library of Congress Cataloging in Publication Data
O'Connor, Edwin.
Benjy: a ferocious fairy tale / by Edwin O'Connor;
illustrated by Catharine O'Neill.
p.   cm.
Summary: Benjy is a very good little boy who never
behaves badly, until a fairy grants him one wish.
[1. Fairies—Fiction. 2. Behavior—Fiction.] I. O'Neill,
Catharine, ill. II. Title.
PZ7.02214Be   1996
[Fic]—dc19   88-46131
CIP
ISBN 0-87923-795-3

First edition
Printed in the United States of America

Chapter 1

Once upon a time, not so very many years ago, there lived in a small town called Smiles, Pennsylvania, a little boy named Benjamin Thurlow Ballou. He had no brothers and no sisters. He lived all alone with his mother, his father, and his doggie. His mother, who was a college graduate, was named Mummy. His father, who was a television repairman, was named Daddy. And his doggie, who was an Airedale, was named Sid.

They all lived together in a nice little house, and they were very happy there.

One night, almost a year after Benjamin Thurlow Ballou was born, Mummy put down one of the big heavy books she was always reading (she called them "texts") and said, "Daddy!"

"Awmpf?" said Daddy. That is, he didn't *really* say "Awmpf," but it *sounded* like "Awmpf" because he was

over on the other side of the room, inside the television set. It was a very big television set, and he often crawled in there to fix wires, or maybe just to have a rest. Sometimes he even took some sandwiches in with him, and a pack of playing cards.

"Do you know what I'm thinking?" said Mummy.

"No dear," said Daddy. He put a red jack on a black queen and took a big bite out of his sandwich. It was a tongue and Swiss cheese on rye bread.

"Come out of there where I can see you!" said Mummy, in a very special voice she sometimes used when talking to Daddy.

Daddy swallowed his mouthful of food very quickly

indeed and poked his head around the corner of the television set. "Here I am, dear," he said.

"That's better. Now then," said Mummy, "I've been thinking about my little Benjamin Thurlow Ballou. His name is lovely but it's too hard."

"Too hard, dear?" said Daddy.

"Not for *me*," said Mummy, looking fondly at her diploma, which was beautifully framed and hanging on the wall. "But there are others around here who haven't had my advantages. I have to think of them."

"Yes, dear," said Daddy. He had no diploma to look at, so all he could do was to look at the television set and hope that Sid the Airedale would not sneak over and grab the rest of his tongue and Swiss cheese sandwich.

———

Fortunately, Sid was doing nothing of the kind. He was lying quietly stretched out in the fireplace catching flies, which is an Airedale's way of having fun.

"Besides," said Mummy, "in a few years now he'll be going to school and the little boys and girls he'll have to play with may very well have trouble with his full name. They may not be very bright. That's why I think we'd better give him some nice little nickname that no one will have any trouble with. I don't suppose *you'd* have any ideas about a nice nickname, would you?"

As these last few words were said in Mummy's very special voice, Daddy thought for a few minutes. Then he said, "How about George?"

"*George*," said Mummy. "I knew you'd say something like that. If some stranger on the street had come up to me and asked me what you'd say, I'd say that you'd say something like *George!*" She looked at her beautiful diploma again and gave a great big sigh. "Well," she said, "at least *one* of us has an idea now and then. I know what we'll call him. We'll call him Benjy."

"Benjy," said Daddy. "That's nice, dear. That's very nice. Benjy."

"All right," said Mummy. "You can go back in your television set now. I'm going up to see my darling baby boy."

And Mummy ran up the stairs and into the bedroom where little Benjy, all wrapped up in his white flannel nightie with the smiling fairies on it, was sound asleep in his little trundle bed. On his beautiful round little face was a smile which said, plain as plain could be, "How I wish I could talk, dear Mummy, so that I could thank you for all the perfect things you've done for me today!"

"My little darling," said Mummy, who was very good at reading smiles. "My little Benjy. Benjy will always be his Mummy's baby boy!"

Meanwhile, downstairs, Daddy was happy, too. All crouched over inside the television set, he was winning at solitaire, he had finished his nice sandwich, and, like his wife Mummy, he was making plans for the future. Tomorrow would be Thursday. Tomorrow night would be a good night to bring a *roast beef* sandwich into the television set, and maybe, too, a little dessert, like a peach, or an apple. That would be fine!

And in the fireplace, Sid was happy. He was counting his flies. He had caught twenty-nine in all: eighteen common houseflies, six bluebottles, and a wasp (which equalled five houseflies). Twenty-nine flies in just two hours and a half. It was better than Sid had ever done before, and he was sure it was very close to being the Airedale record. No wonder Sid was happy!

So then, everybody in the little house was very, very happy, and the happiest of all was little Benjamin Thurlow Ballou, who from now on was to be called Benjy. *He* was so happy because he knew that he was not like bad little boys. He was a good little boy who would sleep the whole night through without waking his darling Mummy even once, or wetting the bed at all.

Chapter 2

Pretty soon little Benjy, who was one of the smartest little boys in the whole wide world, learned to walk and to talk and to play little games that he made up all by himself.

And what nice games they were!

One of the very nicest was one that he played every single morning. Very early, even before Old Mister Sun was up to say, "Good morning, Benjy!" Benjy crept out of his little bed, quiet as a mouse. Then, because he was a good little boy who always did what his Mummy told him, he put on his little pink shoes and his little pink sugarplum bathrobe, and went over to his play box where he kept all his lovely toys.

Oh, how neatly they were put away! Benjy did this all by himself, every night. But now he took all of his wooden building blocks out of the box and brought them over to the floor right next to Mummy's bed. Each building block had a big letter of the alphabet on it, and Benjy took these blocks and right there on the floor he spelled out:

And Mummy, who had been awake all the time, but had just *pretended* to be asleep, reached out and took little Benjy in her arms and snuggled him and covered him with great big kisses.

And Benjy looked up at her with his sweet little smile and said, "I'm very gwad you my Mummy, Mummy!"

And he was only THREE YEARS OLD!

But that wasn't all of the game. Oh no! There was more to come. After all the hugging and kissing was over—and this sometimes took a very long time—Benjy left his Mummy's bed and went back to his blocks on the floor. Then he built a huge big house out of the blocks, way, way up, till it was higher than Benjy himself.

"Benjy's house," he said, giving Mummy another sweet smile. Then his little mouth dropped, and he said, "Poor, poor Benjy. Big house aw faw DOWN!"

And with one little pink shoe he reached out and kicked the house. All the blocks, every single one, came crashing down on the floor with a great CRASH-BANG!

It was a HUGE noise, and it almost scared the life out of Benjy's Daddy, who stayed up late at night, and who had been sound, sound asleep.

"OWP!" he yelled, and he fell out of bed and hit his head, hard, on one of the building blocks that had rolled over near him.

"Goo morning, Daddy dear!" said Benjy, and he ran right across the floor in his little pink shoes and gave Daddy a big kiss, right on the very spot where Daddy's head had hit the building block. "Benjy kiss it and make it aw better," he said.

"Isn't that *cunning?*" said Mummy. She jumped out of bed, ran over and picked Benjy up and gave him a great big squeeze. "That's Mummy's sweet little considerate boy. Well, what do you say to Benjy, Daddy?"

Daddy picked himself up off the floor and rubbed his

head, where it still hurt in spite of Benjy's kiss. "For crying out loud," he mumbled. "It's dark outside. What time is it, for crying out loud?"

"Five-thirty," said Mummy, in her very special voice. "Although I don't see how that has anything to do with it. Kiss your little son good morning. What kind of a father are you, anyway?"

For she was very angry at Daddy, you see. But little Benjy was not. Benjy was not angry at his Daddy at all.

"At's aw wight, Mummy," he said, putting his soft little cheek up against hers. "At's aw wight. Benjy forgive Daddy!"

And this was the game that Benjy played, early every single morning. He had other nice games, too, which he played with his Mummy and his Daddy all day long.

Only Sid the Airedale did not play in any of Benjy's games, because Sid did not live in the house any more. He had moved out into the back yard in the very same week that little Benjy had learned to walk. Here he lived inside a big box marked REFUSE, where he caught a great many flies every day, and was very happy.

Mummy would not let Benjy go near the big box marked REFUSE. She said it was filthy. "Filthy" is a great big word for a very little boy like Benjy to understand, but Benjy was such a smart little boy that he knew just what his Mummy meant.

"Benjy's pwetty wittle hands get all poo-poo," he said, giving Mummy an extra-special big kiss.

And so Sid the Airedale did not see Benjy any more. He just stayed in his box in the back yard and caught flies. Sometimes, at night, when Mummy and Benjy had gone to bed, Daddy would stand all by himself in the dark house, looking out into the back yard at the big box and Sid. And Sid would come out of his box and look back at Daddy.

And no one could tell just what it was they were thinking.

Chapter 3

And now, one day, along came the great morning when everybody in the little house in Smiles, Pennsylvania, woke up from sleepytime with their hearts going flippity-flop, and just as proud and happy as they could be. For today was the day when little Benjy, for the very first time in his whole life, would say good-bye to Mummy and Daddy for the morning and march off to school!

What merry goings-on there were in the little house! And how excited everybody was! Little Benjy was so excited that he almost put on his little union suit inside out. Oh, how he and Mummy laughed at that! And Mummy was so excited that she ripped a great big hole in Daddy's pajamas when she went to hang them on a hook in the closet. And oh, how she and Benjy laughed at *that*! As for Daddy—well, Daddy was so excited about the great day that he sneaked on tiptoe down the back stairs to

the breakfast table and began to eat his boiled egg!

Finally, the moment that everybody had been waiting for arrived: it was time for Benjy to go off to schooldays.

Benjy was all ready. He was all dressed up in his new off-to-school suit that Mummy had bought for him: a beautiful little suit of fudge-colored velvet, with a fine big Buster Brown collar and little short pants that showed the dimples in his knees. No wonder Benjy was such a proud little boy as he marched up and down the room singing, "Happy First Grade to Me!"

Of course Mummy, even though she was very happy, was also very sad, because today would be the first day that Benjy had ever left her, even for just a few hours. But she was a brave Mummy and she told the big tears to go away. Then she came downstairs wearing a big bright smile. And because it was such a great day, and she wanted

everybody to feel oh-so-good, she was also wearing her
college cap and gown.

When Benjy saw his Mummy coming down the stairs,
he jumped up in the air and clapped his hands together,
he was so happy! He had never seen his beautiful Mummy
look so straight and strong and so very much like a Queen.

"Why Mummy," said Benjy, "you're much taller than
Daddy, aren't you?"

"Yes, dear," said Mummy, with a lovely smile. "Much."

"I'll get the car," said Daddy, who was wearing his
corduroy sport coat with the leather elbows.

"Never mind," said Mummy. "Oh no, never mind. Fin-
ish your boiled egg by all means. Your little son starts his
education today but I wouldn't want to interrupt your

boiled egg for that. Besides, I'm going to walk to school with Benjy. We have a great many things to discuss."

And, looking down at Benjy with her special Mummy's eyes, she picked him up in her arms, just as she had when he was a little baby in his nightie with the smiling fairies on it, and began to rock him to and fro and to kiss him, oh, *hundreds* of times.

"On your very first day at school, Benjy dear," she said, "Mummy wants to talk to you just the way Mummy's Mummy talked to her on *her* very first day at school, way, way back before Mummy got her diploma."

And who could wonder, now, if even brave Mummy seemed to sniffle just a wee bit, and if a tiny tear seemed to glisten in the corner of each bright eye? Even Daddy noticed this.

"You got a cold or something, dear?" he asked. "You want the nose drops?"

"Typical!" said Mummy, suddenly looking taller than ever before. "Oh, how typical! *Nose drops!* I hope your little son remembers that. I hope he remembers that on the most important day of a sweet little boy's life, all his father could find to talk about was nose drops!"

"I'll remember, Mummy dear," promised Benjy, and he gave both his Mummy and his Daddy just about the sweetest smile he had ever given them.

––––––

"Well, anyway," said Mummy, adjusting her gown, and fixing her cap so that the tassel came down just so, "it's time for those of us who happen to be interested in our little son's future to be on our way to school. Come along, Benjy dear," she said, taking his hand, "your Daddy will stay here. He'll be right at home going out in the back yard and having another of his nice long talks with that Sid!"

"Good-bye, Daddy dear," said Benjy, running over to Daddy and giving him two very wet kisses on the cheek. Then he ran back to Mummy and said, "Mummy, you know what little Benjy is going to do in school?"

"No dear," said Mummy. "What?"

"He's going to study hard, *hard*," said Benjy, "so some-day he'll get *two* diplomas. Then he can give one to Daddy."

"My sweet little innocent generous boy!" said Mummy, pulling him to her. "Sometimes I want to cry. Come along, now. We don't want to be late, and Mummy has many, many things to tell her little boy on the way."

And so off they went, Mummy and Benjy, hand in hand on their way to Readin' and 'Ritin' and 'Rithmetic.

"Abyssinia," said Daddy after them. "See you Samoa."

This was the way Daddy always said good-bye to people, which made Mummy very angry indeed.

———

Then Daddy went out into the back yard and over to the box marked REFUSE, but he did not talk with Sid the Airedale because Sid was still asleep. Ever since he had moved out of the house and into his box, Sid slept very late in the morning. Then he got up and had fun for the rest of the day, digging up front lawns, stealing bones from smaller dogs, and, of course, catching flies. You might even think, at times, that he did not miss his little friend Benjy at all!

And so Daddy, with no Sid to talk to, just went over and sat by himself on the back steps, and started in counting television aerials. That was a way he had of sometimes having fun.

Chapter 4

What a gay time they had on their way to school that morning! First of all, of course, they had their very, very serious Mummy–Benjy talk, but when this was all over, oh, did the fun begin! Mummy was so excited she was almost like a little girl again, on her way to her own first day at school. In her cap and gown she skipped along the sidewalk beside Benjy, laughing and playing games like "Pease Porridge Hot," and singing her college song.

"Today Mummy's not Benjy's Mummy," she laughed. "Today Mummy is Benjy's little playmate!"

My, but Benjy was proud! Especially when he saw how many people stopped and turned and stared at his beautiful Mummy as she skipped gaily along. He was so proud he felt like jumping up in the air and yelling, "Whee!" And even though Mummy had told him never, *never* to speak to strangers, he was so happy that for just a moment he forgot what his Mummy had told him, and in his happy,

little-boy voice he called out to a man in a white suit who was pushing a big broom.

"Ooo-hoo, Mister Street Sweeper!" he called. "This is my very first day at school!"

But Mister Street Sweeper was not a nice man. Oh no indeed! He was a bad man who needed a shave and who bet on horses and drank coffee.

"Big deal!" he said, in his bad voice. And what was worse, he jerked his thumb at Mummy and said, "Tell that old doll in the black petticoat they'll be comin' for her with a net if she don't cut it out!"

Oh, how lucky it was for Mister Street Sweeper that he disappeared around the corner before Mummy could catch him! For now Mummy was a very cross Mummy. In all his whole life Benjy had never seen her so cross, not even with Daddy.

"Don't be mad, Mummy," said Benjy, putting his little hand in hers and giving a great big squeeze. "Don't be mad just 'cause Mister Street Sweeper said bad things to Benjy!"

And Mummy looked at him with *such* a funny look! Little Benjy had never seen his Mummy look at him like

this before. What could be wrong? Could Mummy be cross with *Benjy*? But no, it was all right, because quick as a bunny the look went away, and Mummy reached down and picked Benjy up and gave him some more good hugs and kisses.

"Mummy's little darling is too young to understand," she said gravely, "but nasty Mister Street Sweeper didn't just say bad things to Benjy. He said some *very* bad things to Mummy, too."

"Oooo, *Mummy!*" said Benjy, and his little robin's-egg-blue eyes got round as saucers. What a good thing it was for Mister Street Sweeper that he was not right there at that moment! How frightened he would have been! For Benjy was so angry that he stamped down hard on the sidewalk with his new patent-leather shoes, and he pushed his little rosebud mouth into such a fierce pout that Mummy almost trembled! And he shook, not one, but *two* little fists at the corner where Mister Street Sweeper had disappeared.

"Oh, *dirty man!*" he cried.

"My sweet brave Benjy!" said Mummy, holding him close. "Defending his Mummy's honor! Oh, how I wish Daddy had seen this! What a lesson it would have been!"

And then, because Mummy was anxious to get away

from this bad place, she took Benjy's hand and off they went to school, just as before. Except that now, for the rest of the way, Mummy neither skipped nor played games. She did not even sing her college song.

Just before they reached the schoolhouse, Benjy stopped and looked up at his Mummy with a very serious face for such a little boy.

"Mummy?" he said softly.

"Yes, Benjy dear?" said Mummy.

"Mummy and Benjy will forgive Mister Street Sweeper, won't they?" said Benjy.

To tell the truth, Mummy had not been thinking of forgiving Mister Street Sweeper at all. She said, "Well . . ."

" 'Cause," said little Benjy, holding Mummy's hand very tightly, "poor Mister Street Sweeper never had a Mummy like my Mummy, did he?"

Never had Mummy been closer to tears!

"How beautiful!" she said, holding Benjy very close. "How beautiful of Mummy's dear sweet little boy. Of course we'll forgive Mister Street Sweeper!"

And as they went into school together, Mummy said happily to herself once again that little Benjy was the best and the smartest little boy in the whole wide world!

Chapter 5

Schooldays, schooldays! At first, how very strange they seemed to Benjy as he sat in the schoolroom without Mummy or Sid or even Daddy. Not that Benjy was a frightened little boy. Oh no! Many of his little classmates were very frightened indeed and did very naughty things, but Benjy did not. He did not cry or sit on the floor and kick or wet his pants. He just sat all by himself at his little desk, smiling down at his beautiful velvet suit, and being happy because nobody else in the whole room looked quite as nice as he did.

Of course Mummy had wanted to be with Benjy in school on this very first day. She had wanted to stay right in the schoolroom with him, holding him on her lap or sitting beside him on his chair. But little Miss Teacher had said, "No no. Mummy!" and so had Mister Principal, and then at last so had Mister School Policeman, who was a very coarse man with a loud voice and dirty fingernails.

And so Mummy had gone out into the schoolyard and found a nice place where, if she stretched way, way up, as far as she could go, she could look right into the schoolroom and see Benjy, smiling at his little suit. What a thrill this was for Mummy on her tiptoes! And how beautiful she looked as she stood there in her cap and gown, tapping at the windowpane and blowing kisses to her Benjy boy!

My, how this surprised Benjy! And how it surprised Miss Teacher! *She* was so surprised that she just stood right in back of her desk for a few minutes, blinking her eyes, before she was polite enough to run out of the room and call back Mister Principal and Mister School Policeman to be part of the nice time.

As for Benjy, he was blowing kisses right back at

Mummy, and his Little-Boy-Blue eyes were just *shining* with happiness. Especially when Mummy would duck her head down below the window sill and then bob up again, as if to say, "Peekaboo, Benjy!" Oh, what fun it was!

Benjy was so happy that he wanted *everybody* to be happy with him, even the dirty little boy at the next desk who had no tie on, and was always doing bad things like sticking his tongue out or pushing his fingers up his nose. Ugh! How disgusting this was to someone with Benjy's lovely manners! But Benjy wanted him to be happy all the same.

"It's all right, dirty boy," he said, in his very nicest voice, "you can blow kisses at my Mummy!"

What a kind thing for Benjy to say! But Mister Bad Manners must have been staying at the dirty little boy's house, because he did *not* blow kisses at Mummy! He did not even smile a thank-you-Benjy smile. Instead he began to make bad noises and terrible faces, and he broke his "I-Am-a-Happy-First-Grader" pencil in his dirty little hands.

"I'll get you, sissy kid!" he growled. "I'll punch you and I'll cut you and I'll make you bleed! You wait!"

These were not very friendly words, but luckily Benjy did not hear them, because he was too busy watching all the other little boys and girls. They were not blowing kisses at Mummy, either, but Benjy could see how happy they were because they were all yelling and laughing and pointing at her, and some of the little boys had even put their thumbs in their ears and were wiggling their fingers at her. What a hit Mummy had made! Benjy felt all happy and toasty-warm all over. Dear Mummy! And good little boys and girls! How glad Benjy was to be in the first grade!

But now Miss Teacher began to shout and to beat on her desk with the nice long ruler she had, and Mister School Policeman ran out of the room and into the schoolyard to say "Hello, Mummy!" to Mummy. And pretty soon Mummy got down from the window and began to march out of the schoolyard, saying loud things over her shoulder to Mister School Policeman, who was marching right behind her. And Benjy and all the other little boys and girls kept watching the window all the rest of the day, hoping that dear Mummy would come back. But she didn't.

Chapter 6

How Benjy enjoyed his trips, early every morning, to The Little Red Schoolhouse! (And here is a little secret: the schoolhouse was *not* little, and it was *not* red! No! It was really a very big building made of gray cement, but both Mummy and Benjy liked to call it The Little Red Schoolhouse.)

Benjy enjoyed going to school so much that he usually ran most of the way. Sometimes he ran so fast that he got way ahead of Mummy, and then Mummy would have to catch up later, all huffy-puffy in her cap and gown. And when they reached the schoolyard, there would be Mister School Policeman waiting for them, smiling his bad smile at Mummy, and swinging his big club ever so slowly. And then Mummy would kiss Benjy 'by-'by for a while and go home. And pretty soon Mummy did not come to school any more at all, but stayed in the little house waiting for

Benjy to come home. And Benjy came home every single day just as soon as school was out, and Mummy met him at the door and said, "My darling little schoolboy!" and gave him lots of big kisses and a special after-school tray of nice jelly sandwiches and milk and cake and Sunshine cookies. And nowhere in Smiles, Pennsylvania—or maybe the whole wide world—was there a happier little schoolboy than Benjamin Thurlow Ballou.

Of all his new friends at The Little Red Schoolhouse, Benjy liked Miss Teacher best. Every morning when she came into the schoolroom, Benjy was standing by her desk, waiting to tell her why he liked her best of all.

" 'Cause you're my School Mummy!" he said. And then, because he was such a kind little boy who wanted to make Miss Teacher the happiest teacher in all the school, he said, "And you're almost as pretty as my real Mummy!"

"Isn't that nice," said Miss Teacher, who was many years younger than real Mummy.

Pretty soon Miss Teacher began to come in earlier and earlier every morning, but no matter how early she came, Benjy was there by her desk with his lovely little smile and the nice words that always put the roses in Miss Teacher's cheeks. Good Benjy!

What a busy little boy Benjy was in the schoolroom! He was so busy you might almost have called him little Benjy the Busy Beaver! And because he did so many things and worked so hard and was so smart, he soon became the very best little pupil in the whole first grade. He always did his lessons and knew the answers, and when all the class recited out loud that A IS FOR APPLE, SO ROUND AND SO RED, Benjy's high clear little voice could be heard above all the rest.

This was especially nice for the first thing every morning, when all the little boys and girls stood up by their desks to recite the Pledge of Allegiance to The Flag of the United States of America, and to The Republic for Which It

Stands. What a wonderful thing it was to hear little Benjy Pledge Allegiance, so much louder than anyone else. How Benjy loved his flag! And sometimes, when Miss Teacher was busy teaching the class, explaining to the little boys and girls that if one cow gave one pail of milk to old Farmer Brown, then *two* cows would give *two* pails, she would hear a little boy's voice talking right out loud in class, and she would look down and see Benjy, standing by his desk like a little soldier with his arms shooting out towards his flag. Pledging Allegiance all over again!

My, how this made Miss Teacher think! She had never seen any of her little pupils do this before. Is it any wonder she told all the other teachers about little Benjy, the very first day? And is it any wonder that Mister Principal himself had Benjy come up to visit him in his big office?

"Well, well, little boy, I think I met your lovely Mummy," said Mister Principal, with a funny smile. He was a very small man with a very big head and not much hair at all. "Now then, I wonder if you can tell Miss Teacher and myself why it is that you Pledge Allegiance so many times each day?"

"Dear Mister Principal," said Benjy, looking at him with his honest little eyes, "it's just 'cause I'm proud to be a little American boy!"

What a pity it was that Mummy was not there at that very moment! How proud she would have been of her little patriot!

And Mister Principal himself was so proud that he stayed in his office for the rest of the day, pulling at the thin hairs on his head, and thinking quite a lot about both Benjy and his Mummy.

Chapter 7

How fine it was for Miss Teacher to have little Benjy in her schoolroom every single day! Besides knowing his lessons and always being the first one to put up his hand whenever Miss Teacher asked a hard, hard question, Benjy also did so many other good-little-boy things that you would almost want to run right into the room and take him by the hand and say, "Oh, how I wish you lived in my house, Benjy boy!"

Of course Benjy loved all his classes, but of them all he liked the music class best. In this class Miss Teacher often sang little songs to the boys and girls. How nice it was for her that Benjy knew so many of these songs by heart, because Mummy had taught them to him! And so Benjy would join Miss Teacher in her songs, and he would not just sing "la la la," but instead he would sing EVERY SINGLE ONE OF THE WORDS! How loudly he would sing! And Miss Teacher, who was used to singing all by herself, and had not expected anyone to help her at all, would be so surprised that sometimes she would sing the wrong notes and then her voice would fade away, and all you could hear would be Benjy. My, how the little boys and girls laughed happily at this! And how Miss Teacher's face got all red with the fun! And Benjy's little smile was never lovelier, because he knew that he had made his School Mummy so happy!

But it wasn't just in music class that Benjy helped Miss Teacher. Oh no! He was always running around the room on his two little legs, helping out. He filled the inkwells and watered the plants and opened the doors and dusted the desks and clapped the erasers and cleaned the blackboards. What a good little blackboard cleaner Benjy was! He was such a good cleaner that he did not even have to be asked. He would march right up to the blackboard and start cleaning away, and sometimes he even cleaned off words and pictures that Miss Teacher had worked hard to put on and had wanted to be left there. When *that*

happened and Miss Teacher would jump up and cry, "Oh, Benjy Ballou!" Benjy would drop his curly little head to one side, put his finger in his mouth, and look up at Miss Teacher with the cutest little look you ever saw.

"Shame, shame on Benjy, School Mummy?" he would say.

And who could be mad at a little boy like that?

What a great help Benjy was to Miss Teacher when it came to his little classmates! For sometimes bad little boys and girls would start whispering when Miss Teacher's back was turned, even though she had warned them not to, because she had eyes in the back of her head and would catch them. But Miss Teacher's back eyes did not seem to work as well as her front ones, because she would have to turn around quickly and ask who had been whispering.

And then do you think the bad little boys and girls would put up their hands and say, "I was the one who was whispering, Miss Teacher?" No, they would not. And if it had not been for little Benjy, Miss Teacher might *never* have known. But Benjy would point them out, one by one, with his little finger. Sometimes Miss Teacher seemed not to see Benjy as he did this, so then he would stand up and tell her right out loud, and then the bad little boys and girls would be kept after school and punished.

Some of the little boys and girls seemed to be very cross with Benjy at this, but Benjy knew that was only because they were bad little boys and girls who could not understand nice boys who loved their teachers.

One afternoon, a very, very bad thing happened to Benjy when he was helping out. School had just finished for the day, and all the little boys and girls were going home, and Miss Teacher was putting things in her pocketbook, when Benjy stood up and said, "Ooh-hoo, Miss Teacher! You forgot something!"

"No, no, I don't think so," said Miss Teacher in a quick voice, because she was hurrying to meet her friend, Mister Man Teacher, in just a few minutes.

"Yes you did, Miss Teacher," said Benjy with a little smile, for lots of times he had to remind Miss Teacher of things she should do. "You told the dirty boy to stay after school for putting chewing gum in the little girl's hair. And he's not staying, Miss Teacher! Look at him going out the door, right now!"

And he pointed his little finger at the door where, just as little Benjy had said, the dirty boy was quietly sneaking out!

And oh, what happened then! The dirty boy made one of his bad noises and turned around and came running back across the room, and what do you think he did? He hit Benjy right in the eye with his dirty little fist!

Oh, what a hard little fist the dirty boy had! And oh, how it hurt Benjy's eye!

"Oh, oh, oh!" cried Benjy, and he fell right down on the floor with his little hand covering his eye! Nothing like this had ever happened to Benjy before! He did not know that he could hurt so much!

"Little Benjy's going to have a bruise!" he sobbed. "Oh, Mummy, Mummy!" And he looked up from the floor to find, not Mummy, but Miss Teacher looking down at him.

"Why, whatever happened, Benjy? she asked, in a pleasant voice.

"The dirty boy," cried Benjy. "He hit little Benjy right in the eye. Didn't you see him, School Mummy?"

"Why, no," said Miss Teacher. "No, I didn't. I didn't see a thing."

And this was very funny, because she had been right there all the time. But maybe she had been turned around and could only see with the eyes in the back of her head.

So Benjy sobbed his little story to Miss Teacher, and Miss Teacher put some cold water on his eye and said that My, my, but we would have to see about this someday, wouldn't we? And then she said 'by-'by to Benjy and ran off with quick steps, for she had something special to tell Mister Man Teacher, her friend.

By the time Benjy got home to his house, how big and puffy and black his eye was! And when Mummy opened the door, she gave a big scream and dropped Benjy's tray of jelly sandwiches and milk and cake and Sunshine cookies right on the floor! Then she fell down on the floor herself, because she had fainted. And when she fell she knocked Daddy's pipe off the table and it broke on the floor in a thousand pieces. It was Daddy's best pipe, the one he took with him into the television set every night. He did not smoke it because he was not allowed to smoke in the house, but he liked to keep it in his mouth anyway.

"For crying out loud," said Daddy, looking down at his broken pipe. "Oh boy. Wow."

After a minute he said that they didn't make pipes like that any more.

Pretty soon Sid came leaping into the house. He had not been in the house for a very long time, and he had just been out having fun tipping over garbage pails, but now he hurried in to look at Benjy's black eye, and to see Mummy on the floor.

After a while Mummy got up and began to hug Benjy and to kiss his eye and to scream at Daddy for not lifting her up faster and to make telephone calls to Mister Doctor and Mister Chief of Police and Mister School Principal and Mister Mayor of the City. My, my, what a busy place the happy little house was all of a sudden!

Poor Mummy! How nervous she was after seeing her baby boy with his big bruise, and after falling down so hard on the floor! And how cross she was because only Mister Doctor came, and Mister Chief of Police and Mister School Principal and Mister Mayor of the City did not! And how *really* cross she got with Mister Doctor because of the way he made fun of little Benjy!

"Run into a doorknob?" he said, and laughed his big doctor's laugh.

She was so nervous and cross that she could only feel better by shouting at Daddy, who was just sitting on a kitchen stool putting pencil ends in his mouth and pretending they were pipes. After a long time Mummy stopped shouting, and Daddy let out all his breath in a great big "A-a-a-h-h!" And then little Benjy came over to Daddy and looked up at him in such a wonderful, melty-tender way that even Sid the Airedale felt like crying big doggie tears and got up and bounded out of the room and did not come back.

"Dear Daddy didn't say he was sorry about poor Benjy's

little eye," said Benjy, in a sad, sad little voice. "Is Daddy still friends with Benjy?"

And this made Mummy start to shout at Daddy all over again. She kept shouting for a very long time until everybody in the little house had to go upstairs to sleepytime.

Just before he climbed into bed, Benjy got down on his little knees to say his prayers. He did this every night, but tonight he was such a very long time that Mummy came over to him and whispered, "Is anything wrong, Benjy boy?"

"No, Mummy dear," said Benjy, and even the terrible black eye could not hide the sweetness of his little smile. "I'm just saying some extra little prayers for the dirty little boy who hit me today."

"Oh!" cried Mummy. "My little saint! Do you hear that, you tobacco fiend?" she said to Daddy. "Doesn't *that* make you feel ashamed of yourself?"

"Yes, dear," said Daddy. "Well, good night, dear."

And he turned over and went to sleep, almost as soon as Mummy had finished talking to him, which was quite a bit later. Then pretty soon Mummy went to sleep and then, last of all, so did Benjy. For Benjy had had a lot to think about for a little boy. What a bad day this had been! Just because he was a good little schoolboy who had tried to help his teacher, he had been given a hard bing-bang, and one pretty little blue eye was now all the way closed and bumpy and black. But while lots of other little boys would have been discouraged by this, and would have said to themselves that from now on they would not help out any more, Benjy was not a bit discouraged, and he did not say anything like this to himself at all. For by the time his other eye had closed, full of the sleepy seeds that Mister Sandman had sprinkled down, a sunny little smile had appeared on Benjy's face, and he said, in a little whisper just loud enough to wake Daddy from his nice sleep, "Tomorrow, School Mummy, I'll help you just the same!"

Chapter 8

And so the days went skipping by, and as they did, the little bluebird of happiness smiled down on Benjy boy all the while. For, although he was still the busiest little boy in the whole school, and helped Miss Teacher as much as ever before, he did not get hit in the eye any more. This was because he no longer helped Miss Teacher with the dirty boy or any of the dirty boy's bad little friends. He had decided to punish those naughty boys by not having anything to do with them at all!

And so he did not join them in their rough games at recess, and he did not say so much as a single word to them, not even when they made their terrible faces at him, and whispered that some day they would get him and punch him and pull his arms and legs off. Benjy just smiled at this like a little gentleman and forgave them. And he never said anything at all about it to Miss Teacher, and so he did not get any more bad eyes.

Just because Benjy would not play with the naughty boys does not mean that he did not have his happy playtime every day. Oh no! He liked to play good games with some of the nice little girls in the first grade, and although some of them were a few weeks or even a few months older than Benjy, it was not long before he was one of the very best in the room at playing Jackstones and Bouncey Bouncey Ball and Ring Around the Rosy. How wonderful it was to watch Benjy as he played Ring Around the Rosey, and to hear his clear little voice piping, "All fall DOWN!" and then to see him tumble to the grass, oh so carefully, so that he would not muss his beautiful velvet suit or give himself a bad bruise! What good fun he had!

Oh, but these were happy days for Benjy, but the very happiest of all did not come until one day when, right out of the big blue sky above, he was given the biggest and most wonderful surprise of his whole little life. On that day, Benjy did something that no other little boy in Smiles, Pennsylvania, had ever done before. He met a Good Fairy!

It happened one afternoon, just after school was over for the day. Benjy was going along, hoppity-skip, on his way home to his Mummy and his jelly sandwiches, when from out of nowhere someone suddenly appeared before him, right there in the middle of the sidewalk. And this was the Good Fairy!

Of course Benjy did not know right away that he had met a Good Fairy, because he had never seen one before. Good Fairies did not visit the little town of Smiles very often, and Benjy had had to learn about them from stories and pictures in his little books. And *these* Good Fairies had not looked at all like the one standing right in front of him on the sidewalk. They had all been pretty ladies with beautiful smiles who floated through the air with wands in their hands and stars over their heads, and had lovely tinkling voices.

But the Good Fairy who was right there in front of Benjy was *not* a pretty lady. No indeed! He was a man: a big fat man with little eyes and a big red bulby nose. And he wore, not lovely robes, but a baseball suit, with a baseball cap tilted to one side of his head. And what do you think he carried in one hand? A wand? No! He carried a big cigar! And when he started to talk, his voice was not at all beautiful or tinkling, but it was loud and hoarse and full of big coughs. So you can understand why it was that little Benjy at first did not quite believe the Good Fairy when he looked down at Benjy and said in his hoarse voice, "Whaddaya say, kid? I'm ya Good Fairy!"

What kind of Good Fairy talk was this? Little Benjy, even though he was a very brave little boy, was almost frightened and began to back away, but the Good Fairy nodded his head and said, "I know, I know. Ya don't belee me. None o' you wise little kids ever do. But look here and I'll prove ya somethin'."

And with that the Good Fairy lifted his cigar up in the air and waved it around, and right before Benjy's wide little eyes, what do you think the cigar changed into? A *baseball bat*! And then the Good Fairy put his other hand up in the air and snapped his fingers, and into the hand popped . . . a *baseball*!

"Okay?" said the Good Fairy. "Now I'll hit a fungo." And he swung his bat and hit the baseball far far away,

right over the tops of the houses. "That woulda been right outa the Stadium," said the Good Fairy. "Center field at that. Well, whaddaya say now, kid?"

And of course, after this, what could a polite little boy like Benjy say except, "Excuse me for not believing you, Mister Good Fairy."

"Okay," said the Good Fairy, waving his arm and changing the baseball bat back into a cigar. "Now less get down ta business."

He pulled an old-looking notebook out of his baseball pants pocket and began to thumb through the pages, and as he did so, little Benjy could not help but notice that not all Good Fairies had very clean thumbs.

"Lessee, now," said the Good Fairy, "you're the Ballou kid, ain't ya?"

The Ballou kid! How very strangely Good Fairies talked!

"Why, Mister Good Fairy," said Benjy, "I'm little Benjy. My full name is Benjamin Thurlow Ballou."

"Okay, okay," said the Good Fairy very quickly, almost

before Benjy had finished what he was saying. Then the Good Fairy gave some big coughs and shook his head, and Benjy could see that his eyes were all watery and red. "Whoo!" said the Good Fairy. "What a night! Never again! Well, anyways, kid, the thing is this: ya got a wish comin' to ya."

"A wish, Mister Good Fairy?" said Benjy. "You mean for being such a good little boy?" For Mummy had told him many times what kind of little boys got wishes granted to them by the Good Fairies, and so now he was not at all surprised.

"Yeah, yeah," said the Good Fairy, just as quickly as before, and making such a terrible face that, if Benjy did not know better, he would almost have thought that the Good Fairy did not really like him at all.

"Nowdays," said the Good Fairy, "it's gettin' so every little crumbcake that goes around blabbin' baby talk and squealin' on the other kids winds up gettin' a wish. It's a real foul-up, Buster, but it ain't none o' my business. I don't shake the dice in this here league: I'm oney the mailman."

And then he stopped because he had to cough his big cough and shake his head some more.

"Whoo!" he said finally. And then he looked at Benjy

with his watery red eyes and said, "Well, whaddaya say, kid? What's ya wish?"

"You mean I can wish for anything I want, Mister Good Fairy?" said Benjy, for that was how it had been in the books.

"Yeah, yeah," said the Good Fairy. "But hustle it up. I can't hang around here all day. I gotta deliver a singin' donkey to some nut kid out in Hollywood. So come on, snap into it. Whaddaya want?"

"I really don't know, Mister Good Fairy," said Benjy, and he looked ever so seriously at the Good Fairy, and put his little finger in his mouth. "All I want is for everybody to love Benjy and be happy."

"That ain't no kinda wish!" shouted the Good Fairy, and he almost seemed cross with little Benjy. "It ain't legal, like. Ya gotta wish for somethin' *special*. Look, I'll help ya. Howja like ta be a big athalete some day? Maybe a big leaguer like the Babe, or Ted Williams? Or," said the Good Fairy, with a modest look, "like *me*? Hey? What's wrong with that, kid?"

"No thank you, Mister Good Fairy," said Benjy, smiling his very politest little smile. "That would be very nice, but my dear Mummy wouldn't want me to grow up and become a baseball man."

"Whoo!" said the Good Fairy, hitting himself hard on the forehead with his hand. "Whoo! What a cornball! Okay then, kid, howsa bout becomin' a fighter? Heavyweight champeen o' the world, maybe? Goin' around drivin' a Caddy, eatin' big steaks, knockin' other guys out: that's the old fun, hey? What kid don't want that?"

"Oh no, Mister Good Fairy!" said Benjy his pretty blue eyes all roundy-wide. "I don't want to hit anybody, ever ever. I just want to be happy friends with people."

"Whoo!" said the Good Fairy again, and he stood looking at little Benjy with his hands on his hips. "I seen some queer ones in this racket, but you take the biscuit, Buster. Okay then, what *do* ya want? Hurry it up. I gotta get out to this little bum in Hollywood before dark, and that ain't no cinch when ya got ya two arms full o' donkey. So come on, kid, spit it out!"

But now little Benjy was all happy-jumpy with excitement, for while the Good Fairy had been talking, Benjy's little brain had been hard at work, saying, "Think think, little Benjy!" and all of a sudden he had had a beautiful idea for the very best wish in the world.

"Oh Mister Good Fairy," he said, "do big and marvelous things happen to good little boys who get wishes?"

"Sure, sure, sure," said the Good Fairy. "Alla time.

Come on, quit stallin'. What's ya wish?"

"Well then," said Benjy, his eyes shining like two little stars, "I make a wish that whatever big and marvelous things happen to little Benjy, the very same big and marvelous things will happen to his dear Mummy, too!"

Who else but little Benjy would have thought of such a beautiful wish as this? And were those tears in the Good Fairy's eyes as he listened to Benjy's little voice? No they were not, but that was only because the Good Fairy was busily working away, writing down Benjy's wish in his notebook. The Good Fairy did not seem to be a very good writer, as he had to print his letters very slowly and kept licking the tip of his pencil with his tongue, but at last he finished and put the notebook back in the pocket of his baseball pants.

BIG AND MARVELLOUS THIr

"Okay, kid," he said. "Toot finee. That's French for Roger Dodger." And, pushing his baseball cap back toward the back of his head, he stood there looking at Benjy for quite a long time.

"Some wish!" he said. "And some kid! Belee me, Buster,

if you was mine I'd put ya behind chicken wire and charge admission!"

But little Benjy did not hear the Good Fairy's funny words, for he was thinking about how nice it was that he was the kind of good little boy who would make such a lovely wish.

"Mister Good Fairy," he said, "will it really come true true?"

"Whaddaya mean, *true true?*" said the Good Fairy. "What kinda talk is that? *True true!* If ya mean are ya gonna get ya wish, the answer is yeah sure. Whaddaya think I come all the way down here for: to fob off phony wishes? The oney thing is, Buster, ya gotta keep ya trap shut. One little word from you about meetin' me today, or about gettin' the wish, and the whole deal's off. That's a rule they got. Don't tell nobody. Understand?"

What a blow this was to Benjy!

"But Mister Good Fairy!" he pleaded. "Not even my *Mummy?*"

"Not even *nobody*," said the Good Fairy. "Or else the wish goes down the drain. What's more, ya'll break out in spots. So be smart, kid, and zip the lip. And now I gotta get outa here if I'm gonna beat the rush hour traffic. So long, kid. See ya in the funny papers!"

And how swift the Good Fairy was, for before Benjy could even say, "I want to thank you, Mister Good Fairy, for the beautiful wish you gave me today!" he was up in the air and out of sight, leaving behind him on the sidewalk only a little cloud of smoke that smelled like old cigars.

And so little Benjy walked the rest of the way home, thinking hard about his wonderful adventure, and about what a bad shame it was that he could not tell his dear Mummy how he had made his wish for her today. But then, before he reached his house, he cheered up, and a sunny smile chased away all the little frowny lines on his face, for Benjy boy was never very long without his little smile, and besides, he knew that Mummy was so clever that someday she would find out who did all the beautiful things for her, and oh, *then* would there be hugs and kisses!

 *Chapter 9*

Was it easy for such a very little boy to keep such a very big secret for the next few weeks? No indeed, not even when the little boy happened to be good boy Benjy. For to tell you the truth, it was really much harder for Benjy, since never in his whole little life had he kept any secrets from his dear Mummy, and now that he had the biggest secret of all he could not tell it to her.

How unhappy this made him feel! Often, in the morning, when he sat at the breakfast table before going off to The Little Red Schoolhouse, he would see Mummy looking at him with her lovely "How-I-Trust-My-Benjy-Boy" look, and then he would feel like crying boo-hoo-hoo into his bowl of Big Boy Crack-a-Pops, and he would almost want to be spanked across the bum-bum.

But he had given his promise to Mister Good Fairy, and because he knew that good little boys kept their promises, and also because he did not want to break out in spots, he did not say one single word about his secret to anybody. And so off he went to school each morning, where he played his happy games with the good little girls at recess, where he was still the smartest little boy in the whole first grade, and where, sometimes, he played a brand-new game with Miss Teacher.

Here is the way he played this new little game. Often, when Miss Teacher would be eating her lunch with the other Miss Teachers at a little table downstairs, Benjy would come in and sit at the table with them and talk with them just like a little grownup. How the teachers would look at each other when this happened, and how quickly Miss Teacher's face would get its pretty red color! Especially when Benjy said nice things about her friend Mister Man Teacher.

"Someday, School Mummy," he would say, "in such a wise little big-man voice that you would want to hug him to pieces, "you and Mister Man Teacher will be Daddy-Mummy, and then you can have a little Benjy all of your very own!"

How all the other teachers would giggle happily at this, and say things like, "That's a good one on you, Bernice!" or "Have you told Clifford the good news yet?" And Miss Teacher would be so pleased that her pretty face would get even redder than before, and her voice would get all shrill and screamy, and, pretending to be cross with Benjy, she would shout at him to get upstairs this very minute! And Benjy, who knew that Miss Teacher was only playing, would get up to go, but first he would smile at her and rub his two little fingers together at her, as if to say, "What I know about Mister Man Teacher and *you*, Miss Teacher!"

Oh, what a little tease Benjy boy was!

But while he had nice fun like this every day at school with Miss Teacher, the most fun of all came every night when he was back in the little house, looking at his darling Mummy, and thinking of all the big and marvelous things that were going to happen soon, all because of his beautiful wish. And sometimes, in spite of what Mister Good Fairy had said, he felt like running right across the room and jumping up into Mummy's lap, and whispering to her, "Know what, Mummy dear? Benjy boy is going to get the *bestest* wish!"

And *one* night he thought so much that he almost did that very thing!

Mummy was in her chair that night, right under her diploma, knitting Benjy a lovely pink sweater with jolly lollipops on it. Daddy was in the television set, all crouched over playing Acey-Deucy. He had a brand-new empty pipe in his mouth, a pack of cards, and an apple. Even Sid was in the house. Sometimes, on cold nights, he liked to come in and play Dead Dog in the fireplace, a good trick which annoyed Mummy very much.

Tonight, however, Mummy did not pay any attention to Sid as he lay in the fireplace on his back with his legs up stiff in the air, for she was very busy talking to Daddy.

"Oh, I know you're in there!" she said, calling over to the television set. "Never mind those nasty quiet shuffles of yours! I hear every single one! I saw you skulk in there with those cards as soon as you got up from the table! I saw you sneak away without so much as one word of appreciation for my lovely dinner! I should know better by this time! I should know better than to feed ho quizzeen to someone half-crazed by tobacco! Live and learn!"

"Yes dear," said Daddy. Then he made another big shuffle and began to deal cards from the *bottom* of the deck. He did this very carefully, for he was practicing cheating.

"Why Mummy," said Benjy, coming over to her, "didn't Daddy like his nice din-din?"

"Don't bother your little head about it, sweet boy," said Mummy. "I don't want to make my little boy any more ashamed of his father than he already is. Did *you* enjoy the din-din, Benjy dear?"

"Mmmm!" said Benjy, smiling and patting his round little stomach. "Num-nummy!"

"Mummy's little boy," said Mummy, smiling back at him. "Just *how* num-nummy?"

"*Num*-num-nummy!" cried Benjy, with a happy little laugh. "Oh, Mummy-Mummy-Mummy, it's num-num-nummy!" And then, because he was so happy, without even thinking of what he was saying, all of a sudden he said, right out loud, "It's almost as num-num-nummy as my very own beautiful wish!"

His very own beautiful wish! Just as soon as he had spoken little Benjy realized what he had done, and he clapped his two little hands over his mouth just as fast as fast could be. But it was too late: he had already said the bad words. *Now* what would Mister Good Fairy do? Would he punish Benjy, hard hard? Or had he heard what Benjy had said? Maybe—just maybe—Mister Good Fairy had been far far away, deliverying more singing donkeys, and had not heard a single word! But even while Benjy was thinking this, suddenly there came into the room a strong bad smell of old cigars, and now Benjy started to shake in his little patent-leather shoes (size 4½) for he knew that Mister Good Fairy was nowhere delivering singing donkeys but was right here in the room with him!

"Oh please please please, Mister Good Fairy!" he cried. "Benjy's sorry! Benjy didn't mean it! Don't make little Benjy break out in spots! Please please, Mister Good Fairy, just one more chance for Benjy boy!"

Goodness knows what Mummy would have thought if she heard her little boy talking like this! And especially to someone she could not even see! But fortunately Mummy did not hear Benjy for she was not listening. Instead, she was standing in front of her chair with her sharp nose high in the air, sniffing the bad cigar smell and saying, "Aha! Aha!" For Mummy did not know about Mister Good Fairy and thought that the cigar smell came from somewhere else.

"All right!" she shouted at the television set. "You've gone too far this time! I knew you would! Give you an inch and you'll take a mile! At last you're caught red-handed, aren't you? Come out of there this instant!"

And slowly Daddy came out of the television set with a funny look on his face, for he thought that Mummy had found out about his new way of playing cards.

"Hello, dear," he said. "Just a little bottom deal, dear. A little fun, that's all. I'm not playing for money in there. There's only me."

"Only you!" said Mummy. "Oh yes, only you! Only you and your cigar, you mean! You wouldn't forget *that* little friend, would you? The one that's made a smokehouse out of my lovely living room?"

"Cigar, dear?" said Daddy. "You mean my pipe, dear? My empty pipe? I don't have any tobacco, dear."

"Don't play dumb with me!" said Mummy. "We've gone too far for those tricks! I've been too good to you, that's my trouble! You've been spoiled! And now in return for my kindness I'm expected to live with my little son in a room that positively reeks of poison! Just smell this filthy air! Go ahead, take a *deep* breath!"

And so Daddy took a deep breath of the cigar smell. Then he took another and another and another. He took lots of deep breaths.

"Ah," he said. "Oh boy."

"I'll oh boy you," said Mummy, coming over to him and standing in front of him, straighter and taller than ever before. "All right," she said. "Hand it over! Give me that cigar this very second!"

"But dear," said Daddy, "I haven't got any cigar. Honest to Pete."

"No, of course you haven't!" said Mummy. "I suppose *I'm* the one who's been smoking! Or your little son! Or that silly dog lying there in the fireplace with his feet up in the air!"

And with this Sid, who was a sensitive Airedale, got right up out of the fireplace and marched out of the room,

without barking once or even so much as looking to either
side of him.

"Here boy," said Daddy, but not very loudly.

"Never mind," said Mummy, going behind the television
set. "I'll find it myself! I'll let your little son see his Daddy
exposed in a lie right before his very eyes! Won't that be
a fine example for a little boy?"

And she got down on her hands and knees and crawled
into the television set and started throwing out Daddy's
things. She threw out the pack of cards, his new empty

pipe, an apple core, some old raisins, a pencil stub, and a used-up match box that Daddy had found marked "Paradise Isles." But she did not throw out any cigar.

After a while she crawled back out of the television set with her face all red and mad and her hair all out of place and her dress all rumpled.

"All right!" she said, jumping to her feet and standing almost on top of Daddy. "Empty out your pockets! All of them!"

"Okay dear," said Daddy.

And Daddy emptied his pockets very quickly, for he did not have much in them. He had a handkerchief, a little wallet, a fingernail clippers, a peppermint Life Saver, and twenty-three cents. But he did not have a cigar.

"Oh, you're sly!" said Mummy. "I admit that. You have a kind of cunning! But I'll find you out. I'll find you out if it takes all night!"

And she began to talk even louder to Daddy, still standing close to him, and she talked and talked for a very long time.

And all the time Mummy and Daddy were having their little talk, Benjy was not listening to them at all, but was standing right in front of the big mirror, looking at himself with unhappy eyes, and waiting for his spots to break out!

Poor Benjy! He did not even know how big his spots would be, or if they would be bad colors. All he knew was that they would cover him all over and then he would not be Pretty Benjy any more, but he would be Ugly Benjy. And all his little playmates at school would laugh and point at him and say, "Ooo-hoo, Spotty Boy!" Is it any wonder that Benjy almost wanted to lie right down on the floor and cry a little round warm pool of tears?

But after a few more minutes Benjy began to feel better. Because, although he kept looking at himself in the mirror

hard hard, he could not see one single spot! And maybe, thought Benjy, this meant that Mister Good Fairy was not going to punish him after all! For while Benjy *had* told Mummy that he had a wish, he had *not* told her what kind of wish it was, and he had not told her about Mister Good Fairy. So he had really not given away his secret after all! And maybe Mister Good Fairy had just given him a little warning with the bad cigar smell, and was not going to take his beautiful wish away or make him break out in spots! Oh, how good this would be! It would be the very best num-num-nummy of all!

And sure enough, that was the way it turned out. For pretty soon the bad cigar smell went away, and Benjy went softly up the stairs and into his little room and there was still not a single spot anywhere to make him an ugly boy. So he put on his little nightie and dropped off to sleepytime with a happy smile on his face, after first thanking Mister Good Fairy and promising him that he would never never again say anything about his beautiful wish, not in his whole little life. Then he closed his little eyes and began to dream nice dreams about himself that were sweet as chocolate-covered cherries. That is what little Benjy's dreams were like.

While downstairs, Mummy was busy shaking Daddy. After a while she stopped shaking him and began to play a game called Cigar Hunt. She took Daddy by the hand and pulled him upstairs and downstairs and through every room in the house, but they did not find any cigars. Then Mummy began to talk again and shake her head and wave her arms, and then at last she said good night, Daddy.

"Watch out!" was the way she said it. "That's all I have to say to you! Just watch out!"

"Yes, dear," said Daddy. "Good night dear."

Then everybody went fast asleep and they slept through the rest of the night, except for a few times when Mummy, who had a nice memory, remembered some things she had forgotten to say to Daddy.

But out in the backyard, Sid did not go to sleep at all. He sat in the doorway of his house marked REFUSE, looking at the moon, and making paw marks in the dirt like this:

Which, in dog language, means, "I may be only a dog, but I have feelings."

And he stayed up all night and thought a lot about Mummy.

Chapter 10

And, during the next few weeks, how many times do you think that big and marvelous things happened to little Benjamin Thurlow Ballou and his darling Mummy? Fifty times? Ten times? Five times?

No. *No times.* No times at all.

How very strange this seemed to Benjy! For he knew that, though he had always been a lovely little boy, ever since he had made his wish he had been even lovelier. In school, he had helped Miss Teacher so much that there was not a single minute of the day when he was not right by her side. Even when she went to meet her friend, Mister Man Teacher, to go for their little walks together, Benjy would go along too, and he would keep right up with them, even when they walked fast fast. What a scowly face Mister Man Teacher had on these walks! He was so scowly that there were times when little Benjy almost thought of not helping him any more.

And at home, Benjy helped his dear Mummy more than ever before. Every morning he woke up singing like a happy little robin, and he woke everybody else from sleepytime with his nice first grade songs like "The Goldenrod Is Yellow" and "Bunny's Tracks Are in the Snow." Then he would help Mummy get the breakfast. Benjy was such a good little cook that pretty soon Mummy let him make Daddy's coffee every single morning. And what good coffee he made! It was scarcely brown at all! By the time he was ready to march out the front door for the Little Red Schoolhouse, he had helped out so much that Mummy could not help hugging him and kissing him and saying in a very loud voice that it was nice to have a man in the house at last!

But even though he had been so extra-special good, nothing big or marvelous had happened. Whatever could the matter be? Of course Benjy was too good to think bad things about Mister Good Fairy and his big friends up in the sky, but sometimes he almost wondered if Mister Good Fairy had not told him a fib! But he did not wonder this very much, because as soon as he did the bad cigar smell would come back into the room very quickly, and Mummy would jump out of her chair and start shouting at Daddy again, and Benjy knew that Mister Good Fairy was there. Then Benjy would be frightened and he would whisper very fast, "Little Benjy believes you,

Mister Good Fairy! Honest and true true!"

And pretty soon the bad cigar smell would go away, but even when it had gone, nothing big or marvelous happened; and the days went by, one after another, and still nothing happened, and all of a sudden it was time once again for Daddy's Birthday Picnic.

What a great day this was in the little house! How Mummy and Benjy loved picnics, and what a treat it was when, every year, they all went off on a picnic on Daddy's Birthday! It was not quite as big a treat for Daddy, because he did not really like picnics very much, but he had to go because this was Mummy's special birthday present every year.

So off they drove in their little car, with Mummy up in front in the driver's seat, with little Benjy by her side, and Daddy sitting all by himself in the back with the lunch basket.

"You don't deserve it this year," Mummy said to Daddy, talking back over her shoulder, "because of those cigars! I hope you realize how lucky you are, going off on a nice time like this in spite of everything! Don't touch that lunch basket!"

"No dear," said Daddy, although to tell the truth he had been just about to peek in under the cover, for he was very hungry. "We got a nice lunch today, dear?" he said.

"We have no cigars, if that's what you're driving at," said Mummy. "No, I'm afraid I didn't include any of your famous filthy cigars on our luncheon menu today. But for those of us who can manage to exist for five minutes without tobacco, it will be a delicious lunch. We'll have all the usual sandwiches: cucumber, egg salad, tuna fish, and peanut butter and jelly. And of course what my baby boy likes best in all the world: toasty marshmallows!"

"Oh, Mummy!" cried Benjy, "Mmmmm!"

"Joy joy, little Benjy?" said Mummy, giving him a fond little squeeze.

"Joy joy, Mummy!" said Benjy, smiling up at her.

"And," said Mummy, talking to Daddy, who was

looking very hungry, "there happens to be an extra surprise for you this year. I just hope that you can appreciate it. Your little son had brought along a big Thermos bottle filled with the coffee he makes especially for you!"

"Oh boy," said Daddy very quietly. "Wow."

What a Happy Birthday Picnic it was going to be for Hungry Daddy!

And pretty soon Mummy turned the little car off the main road, and up another road, and then they reached the Picnic Place. This was a lovely meadow with plenty of big rocks and trees, just halfway up the side of Mount Laugh, which was the only mountain in Smiles, Pennsylvania. And when they got there, who shoud be waiting for them but Sid!

Sid knew where they went every year on Daddy's Birthday, but he liked to get there first to fix his own lunch, for he was only a dog and did not like the kind of nice food Mummy brought. And how Daddy looked at Sid's big pile of bones with the pieces of meat still on them! Funny Daddy! Whatever was he thinking?

Then Daddy carried the lunch basket over to a side of the Picnic Place which was far away from the other people who had come up to picnic, or maybe just to walk around, but whom Mummy did not like because they were common. And how beautifully Mummy and Benjy ate their sandwiches with their lovely manners! But how strange it was to watch Daddy eat his in great huge bites, swallowing them very quickly almost as if he did not want to taste them!

"Happy Birthday, Daddy dear!" said little Benjy, running up to him and pushing something small and wrinkly and black at him on the end of a stick. "Here's a pretty toasty marshmallow for my Daddy!"

"Owp!" cried Daddy, for Benjy put it right in his mouth for him, and it was all very hot and hard and gave his tongue a very bad burn. "For crying out loud," he said.

"Pull in your tongue this second!" said Mummy. "A grown man sitting there with his tongue lolling out! What will people think of me? And drink your coffee!" she said, pointing to the Thermos bottle, which Daddy must have forgotten because he had not even touched it. "Stop whimpering and drink the coffee your little son was good enough to prepare for you with his own little hands! At least try to act like a decent parent on your birthday!"

"Benjy gave up his playtime to make Daddy's Happy

Birthday coffee, didn't he, Mummy?" said Benjy, with a tender look.

"Sweet boy!" said Mummy, patting his cheek. "Indeed he did. And Daddy is going to drink his Happy Birthday coffee, every single drop, just to show his little son how much he appreciates it. All right!" she said in her special voice to Daddy. "Drink up!"

So Daddy drank his Happy Birthday coffee, mostly in great big gulps, stopping to put his tongue out in the air to cool whenever Mummy was not watching him, which was not very often. And Benjy watched his Daddy drink coffee for a while, and then he got up and began to run around and play by himself over by some big rocks at the far far edge of the Picnic Place.

All of a sudden Mummy was interrupted in her watching of Daddy by a big yell from the far far edge, and she quickly turned around to see little Benjy jumping up and down and waving his arms and yelling, "Mummy! Mummy!"

"A rattlesnake!" cried Mummy, leaping up. "My own little boy had been bitten by a rattlesnake! I know it! Get up on your feet!" she shouted at Daddy. "Your little son is dying of rattlesnake bites and you sit there like a lump swilling down your precious caffeine!"

"But dear," said Daddy, pulling in his tongue to talk, "how could he get bit by a rattlesnake? I mean, there's no rattlesnakes around here, dear. There's never been. Holy smoke, dear."

"Don't use you oaths with me!" said Mummy. "I'll holy smoke you!" And, reaching down, she pulled Daddy to his feet so fast that he spilled quite a bit of his Happy Birthday coffee all over himself. "You'll come along with me and save your dying son whether you want to or not!" said Mummy.

And, pulling him after her, she ran across the Picnic Place to her Benjy boy. As she ran, she reached over and tore Daddy's new birthday tie right off his neck.

"A tourniquet!" she cried. "We'll need a tourniquet!"

But when they reached little Benjy, they found they did not need a tourniquet at all, because he had not been bitten by a rattlesnake at all! He had not even been bitten by *anything*! He was shouting and jumping up and down, not because he was sick, but because he had found something so exciting that he had to show it to his dear Mummy right away! But Mummy was so happy to see her Benjy without any rattlesnake marks and not all swollen up and blue that he could not show her anything at all until she had picked him up in her arms and covered him with lovely Mummy kisses.

Then, when all the good kissing was over, Benjy took Mummy by the hand and they ran fast fast to see what he had found. Daddy came too, only not so fast, because he still had a sore tongue, and then after Daddy came Sid, who was slowest of all because he had eaten such a big lunch.

And what do you think it was that Benjy had found, all by himself, hidden away in the big bare rocks at the far far edge of the Picnic Place? A secret cave? A pirate treasure? A space ship? No. He had found . . . a NEST! A *bird's* nest! But it was not in the least like an ordinary bird's nest, which is little and neat and made of twigs and mud and bits of string. *This* nest was huge and very untidy, and made of rough branches and hunks of rope and even pieces of wire. You might even think it had not been made by a bird at all, except that right in the middle of it was . . . an egg! And what an egg! It was about as big as a coconut, and it was a shiny black color, with one bright

red spot on one end and one bright green spot on the other! And for just a moment everybody looked at the nest and then at the egg and they could not even say a single word!

"Boy," said Daddy at last. "Boy. How'd that egg be all boiled up for breakfast, hey?"

"Predictable!" said Mummy, putting her hand over her eyes. "Forever the Philistine! You've never heard of the word 'beauty,' have you? You can't begin to realize that your little son has discovered something rare and lovely, can you? Boiled up indeed!"

"It's all cold, Mummy dear," said Benjy, who had gone over to the nest and was stroking the egg with one hand. "It feels all cold to my little touch."

"That's because it's an *abandoned* eggie, sweet boy," said Mummy. "That means there are some Mummy birds who are very bad Mummy birds who don't love their little eggies, and who fly away and leave them so that they can never hatch into lovely chickabiddies."

"Boy," said Daddy, giving a little laugh. He did not laugh very much but when he did it was a coarse little laugh that always made Mummy ashamed of him. "Boy," he said, looking at the big egg, "I'd sure hate to meet the chickabiddy that hatched from *that* egg. Some real king-size chickabiddy."

Then, seeing the way Mummy was looking at him, he said, "Just a little joke. It's a nice egg. A real pretty egg. It sure took a whopper of a bird to lay that pretty egg." And then Daddy suddenly looked up over his shoulder into the sky just a little bit uneasily and said, "Maybe she's still hanging around. Behind a cloud or something. Maybe we ought to get out of here, dear."

"A craven!" said Mummy. "I've married a craven! And of course you want us to leave the egg behind! You're all for giving up this precious jewel of an egg that your own little son was the first to discover, aren't you? Of course you are! That's my husband! I'm the only woman in the world married to a man who's afraid of an egg!"

"Oh Mummy dear!" cried Benjy, in his very special sad-little-boy voice that almost made Mummy want to burst right into big tears, and even made Sid the Airedale want to stuff his ears with dirt and pound his head hard on the ground. "Oh Mummy dear, don't take Benjy's eggie away! It's not the Mummy bird's eggie any more! It's little Benjy's eggie now!"

"Don't worry, sweet boy," cooed Mummy. "Of course Benjy can keep his eggie. Mummy and Benjy will take the pretty eggie back home to the little house no matter what fraidy-cats say!"

"Oh Mummy!" said Benjy, clapping his hands. "And maybe Benjy and Mummy can *hatch* the pretty eggie! They can take turns! Then we will have a little Benjy-bird!"

"Oh, he has his Mummy's imagination!" said Mummy happily. "The divine spark! I only hope he doesn't make the same sorry mistake his Mummy made! Just see to it, sweet boy, that you don't throw away your gifts as I've thrown mine! I've given the best years of my life—"

"Hey hey hey!" said Daddy suddenly, interrupting Mummy. He almost never interrupted Mummy, but he interrupted her now. "Hey," he said, looking anixously at

Benjy, "no kidding. You better put that thing down."

For Benjy had put his two little hands underneath the pretty egg and was lifting it right out of the nest!

"Once and for all, YOU LEAVE THAT SWEET LIT-TLE BOY ALONE!" said Mummy talking in her through-her-closed-teeth voice. "Don't try to infect him with your silly fears! Don't try to make a craven out of my son!"

"I'm a brave little boy, aren't I, Mummy?" said Benjy with one of his brightest smiles. "And now I have my very own eggie, and the bad old Mummy birdie hasn't got it any more!"

"Hey hey hey!" said Daddy suddenly, in the loudest voice he had ever used. "WATCH IT!"

For something was happening! The pretty egg was very heavy, much *much* heavier than it looked and Benjy, when he started to carry it across to his dear Mummy, found that it was so heavy he could not hold it tight at all! And it began to slip, and the next thing you know it had slipped right out of Benjy's hands and crashed down onto a big rock at his feet.

"BONG!" it went.

It did not sound like an egg at all! It sounded like a great mad gong! Then it bounced straight up in the air two times and each time it came down on the rock again it made the same sound.

"BONG! BONG!"

It was a sound you could hear for miles! And then it bounced up in the air once more, and this time, when it came down, it did not go "BONG!" but it broke on the rock and split all apart, and a great black yolk came spilling out, covering the ground in a big inky pool!

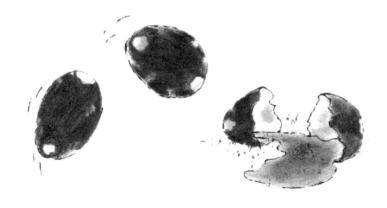

"Wow!" said Daddy, and he was the only one who said a word. Mummy and Benjy just stood there with their eyes wide open and their mouths wide open, and Sid went and hid behind a rock.

Then, suddenly, they heard a noise. It was a high, whistling noise from somewhere up in the sky, like the noise of a jet plane shooting by. And Mummy and Benjy and Sid and Daddy all looked up together, buy they did not see any jet plane. They did not see anything special at all: just a few clouds, and the bright, shining, midday sun.

But the noise grew louder and louder, and suddenly, while they were all still looking up, they saw what seemed to be a dark speck in the sky, coming over the top of the mountain. It was coming towards them, and it was coming very very fast. It was coming so fast that even before they could blink their eyes to make sure that the speck was really 'there, it had become ten times bigger and darker, and was now a long black streak, shooting down across the face of the sun and making a big shadow on the ground!

"Oh oh!" cried Daddy, for he had wonderful eyes, even for a television repairman, and saw what it was before any of the others did. "It's the big bird! Wow!"

And indeed it was a big bird! It was an enormous black bird with even blacker wings which flapped up and down very slowly, but which drove it forward at a furious speed! It came nearer and nearer and nearer, and when it was still high in the sky, but directly over the heads of Mummy and Benjy and Sid and Daddy, it seemed to stop still and

fold its great wings to its sides, and the loud whistling noise became quiet. There was a second of terrible silence, and then the big bird seemed to tilt slowly forward, and all of a sudden it began a swift, roaring, rushing dive, right down upon them!

And it was now that little Benjy who was one of the smartest little boys in the whole first grade began to suspect that something might happen to him.

"Oh Mrs. Mummy Bird!" cried Benjy. "No! No! No! Don't touch little Benjy! Don't give him a bruise! He didn't break the pretty eggie! He didn't even touch it! Honest and true true! Some bad boy did! Don't be cross with little Benjy, Mrs. Mummy Bird! Oh please please PLEASE!"

But it was too late, for Mrs. Mummy Bird, who by now was very close to them, looked very cross indeed! She had a long, dark-red beak which was curved like a Turkish sword and great red flaming eyes as big as traffic lights and huge red talons which she was lowering slowly from her feathers like a giant landing gear! But she did not land at all! Instead, just as she almost reached the ground, her great wide wings snapped out, her great red talons shot forward, and with a swift WHOOSH she flew by so low that Daddy got a long black feather in his mouth, and she picked little Benjy right off the Picnic Place as neatly as if he were a piece of lint and flew off with him into the sky!

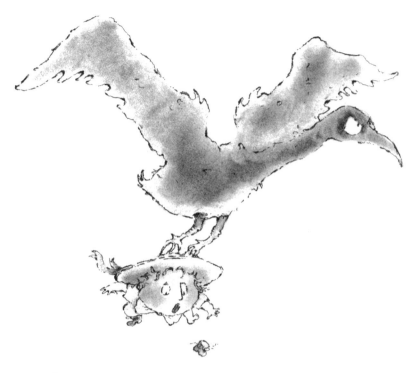

"Oh Mummy Mummy Mummy!" cried Benjy, kicking his fat little legs and struggling to get free. But he could not, for the Mummy bird's great talons were firmly caught in his beautiful suit of fudge-colored velvet which Mummy had bought for him. It was a lovely suit of the nicest, very strongest material, and as it was so strong, it was naturally very good for carrying little boys off in.

"Save me, Mummy, save me!" cried Benjy, his little voice getting fainter and fainter in the distance.

"Mummy's coming, sweet boy!" screamed Mummy. "Mummy's coming!"

And how funny Mummy looked as she stood there on the Picnic Place with her head shooting forward and her feet wide apart and her arms flapping at her side, almost as if she were trying to fly!

"Never fear!" she cried. "Mummy's on her way!" And, strange as it seems, so she was! For, even as little Benjy was being carried off, *another* whistling noise had started overhead, and even though they did not hear it at first, now Daddy and Sid looked up to see *another* bird, bigger and blacker than the first, diving down upon them!

"Oh boy!" shouted Daddy. "Hit the dirt, everybody!" And Daddy hit the dirt, and so did Sid, fast. But Mummy did not. She was too busy flapping her arms, trying to get off the ground. And the big bird, with his great red beak and his great red eyes and his great red talons, came rushing past with another WHOOSH, and as he passed it was clear that he must be the Daddy bird, because of the big

tuft of feathers on his head which was shaped like a derby hat! And just as the Mummy bird had picked off little Benjy, so did the Daddy bird pick off Mummy and carry her, struggling and screaming into the sky!

And up up up they flew, with the Daddy bird flying so fast that he soon caught up with the Mummy bird, and together the Mummy bird, the Daddy bird, little Benjy and Mummy flew into the face of the bright sun, over the top of the mountain, and completely out of sight!

And then everything was very still.

After a while, Daddy got up off the ground, and so did Sid. They stood for a little, looking into the sky, and at the top of the mountain. Then Daddy spoke.

"Wow," he said.

After a minute he lifted his head and began to sniff.

"Cigars," he said.

And it was true—the air was full of the strong smell of

old cigars! And of course Daddy did not know, and Sid did not know, what this meant: that Mister Good Fairy was right there with them, and had been for some time, watching little Benjy Boy's wish at last come true!

For, finally something big and marvelous had happened to Benjy, and surely no one would not agree that it is a big and marvelous thing to be the only little boy in Smiles to be captured by the biggest bird that ever was! And because of his wish, that whatever big and marvelous thing happened to him would happen to his Mummy too, Mummy also had been captured and taken away! And if it had not been for her little boy's beautiful wish, Mummy would never have had this big marvelous thing happen to her, and she would still be standing, flapping her arms, on the Picnic Place!

And the Good Fairy, who was sitting there invisible on a high rock, with his baseball cap tilted down over his eyes to keep out the bright shining midday sun, knew all this and puffed contentedly on his short black cigar with the air of a Good Fairy who has done his work well. Then he pulled the tattered notebook out of his baseball pants pocket and wrote, with his stubby pencil, one last sentence under the name BALLOU, Benjamin Thurlow. Then he put the notebook and pencil away and leaned back comfortably, with his arms behind his head, and sighed.

"Toot finee," he said, and blew a big cloud of smoke.

But Daddy and Sid, who did not know any of this, just stayed around for a few minutes more, and then went home, after first getting away from some of the people who had been at the Picnic Place and who had seen what had happened and who were anxious to ask Daddy questions. But Daddy did not say anything much, and neither did Sid.

And that night, in the living room of the little house,

Daddy and Sid sat all alone, watching television. Daddy did not sit inside the television set now. He sat in the big comfortable chair with the footstool in front of it. At his right hand, on a little table, was a big can of beer which he was pouring into a nice cold glass. On the floor, near Daddy's feet, lay Sid. He was all stretched out with his muddy paws making a few marks on the rug every now and then. Under his head was a satin pillow which was one of Mummy's favorite pillows. On it she had embroidered: A BOY'S BEST FRIEND IS HIS MUMMY!

So Daddy and Sid just stayed there, watching television for a while, because the man on television was a newsman who was talking about Mummy. He was a bald man with a big mouth and sad eyes.

"Yass," he said, "oh yass, dear friends, a tragic story tonight. Mummy Ballou, college graduate, and her little son, Benjy Ballou, birdnapped from a lovely recreation ground in the little town of Smiles, Pennsylvania! Tragic for everyone, but especially tragic for the lone survivor, Daddy Ballou, respected television repairman in that little community! Tonight the hearts of all America go out to that lonely man who, bathed in melancholy most profound, sits alone in his living room, sorrowing, sorrowing, sorrowing. . . ."

And Daddy and Sid watched for a little while more, and then Daddy got up and switched channels and got a Wild West program, the star of which was a hero dog. How Daddy and Sid enjoyed this program! Daddy had a drink from his glass, and then he lit up a very long and quite expensive cigar and started puffing.

"Ah," he said, and sighed a long sigh. Then he said, "Have a beer, Sid?"

Sid shook his head no, but with his paws he thumped the floor in a way which meant, "I like it, but it doesn't like me!"

"Okay," said Daddy, and puffing once more at his cigar, he settled back to enjoy the Western. He spent almost the whole night like this. Every once in a while he had another little drink from his big glass, and then he lit up another cigar, and then he thought, quite often, of Mummy and Benjy. He thought of the strange way in which they had gone away, and he wondered whether they would ever come back. On the whole, he thought, it was very very possible that they would never come back.

And they never did.